DATE DUE			
SEP 20			
OCT 18 1992			
MAR 05			
MAR 13 1996			
JAN 29 1997			
NOV 11			

F
BAK

Baker, Barbara.

Oh, Emma.

LAKESHORE ELEMENTARY SCHOOL
HOLLAND, MI   49424

Oh, Emma

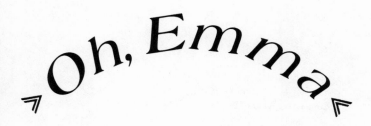

Oh, Emma

by Barbara Baker

illustrated by Catherine Stock

DUTTON CHILDREN'S BOOKS   NEW YORK

Library of Congress Cataloging-in-Publication Data

Baker, Barbara, date.
  Oh, Emma / by Barbara Baker; illustrated by Catherine Stock.—
1st ed.
    p.   cm.
  Summary: Frustrated by life in a crowded housing project, Emma
longs for a room of her own but, because of family circumstances,
must settle for far less.
  ISBN 0-525-44771-7
  [1. Family life—Fiction.   2. Apartment houses—Fiction.]
I. Stock, Catherine, ill.   II. Title.
PZ7.B16922Oh   1991   91-2578
[Fic]—dc20   CIP
                                                               AC

Published in the United States by
Dutton Children's Books,
a division of Penguin Books USA Inc.

Designer: Carol McDougall

Printed in U.S.A.   First Edition
10 9 8 7 6 5 4 3 2 1

For my mother, my father,
Jeanne and Chip
B.B.

For Susan
C.S.

Emma and Janie Tucker sat at their kitchen table working on scrapbooks. They had a big pile of old magazines.

"If you save houses and dogs for me," said Emma, "I'll save beautiful ladies for you. Okay?"

"Okay," said Janie. "Beautiful ladies are the best."

Emma turned a page in her magazine. Outside, rain streamed down the kitchen window. It had been raining all day—the kind of rain that made everything soggy and gray, but didn't cool things off.

It felt wet indoors too. Hot and wet and sticky. The first-floor apartment where Emma lived felt just like a steamy jungle. She wondered if all of the apartments in the housing project were as hot as hers. Maybe the upstairs ones got a breeze.

Emma looked over at Janie's scrapbook. It was a mess. But Janie couldn't help it. She was only six. She never did anything right.

Emma was nine. She looked at her own scrapbook. It was almost perfect. She had been working on it all summer.

"You're using too much glue," Emma told Janie. "That's why your pictures look squishy."

"They do not," said Janie.

"Yes they do. And anyway, Mommy says you shouldn't waste glue. It's expensive." Emma looked at the page Janie was working on. "And you're cutting out pictures of everything. It's better if you just do pictures of things you really like."

"I *do* like all of these things," said Janie. "You leave me alone, or I'll tell Mommy." She pasted some vegetables next to a picture of a tube of toothpaste.

"I was just trying to help. You don't

have to be such a baby.
through the pages of anothe
stopped at a picture of a be
beautiful. Everything was blu
There was even a canopy on the
just the kind of room Emma wo   if
her family ever moved into a h use. She
started to cut.

"Hey," said Janie. "There's a lady in
that picture. You said I could have all the
ladies. You *said.*"

Emma stopped cutting. There *was* a lady
in the picture. She was sitting on the bed.
"You can't have this lady," said Emma. "If
I cut her out, the bedroom will be ruined,
and bedrooms are part of houses, and *I* get
houses."

"That's not fair," yelled Janie. She
grabbed the magazine from Emma. There
was a ripping sound.

"Now look what you did," said Emma.
She took the picture that Janie had been
cutting out—a lady putting red lipstick on
her lips. She tore the picture in half.

"Mommy!" Janie screamed.

"What's going on in here?" Mrs. Tucker came into the kitchen. "Can't I leave you two alone for five minutes?"

"It's Janie's fault," said Emma.

"She ripped my beautiful lady," said Janie.

Mrs. Tucker pointed to the pile of magazines. "Look," she said. "There are plenty of magazines for both of you. If you're going to fight over them, you can just put them away right now and find something else to do. Do you hear me?"

"We'll stop fighting," Emma said. She didn't want to put her scrapbook away.

"Good," said her mother. "And please keep your voices down. I just put Nick in for his nap. I want to try to get some things done while he's sleeping."

"Okay," said Emma.

"Okay," said Janie.

Emma waited until her mother left the room. "You're just a tattletale," she whispered to Janie. "It's your fault Mommy yelled at us."

"It is not," said Janie. "You said I could have the beautiful ladies. You promised."

"You and your dumb ladies. You always spoil everything." Emma picked up the torn picture of the bedroom. Maybe she could fix it with tape. No. It was a mess. "Here," she said to Janie. "You can have it."

Janie glued the bedroom down onto the page with the vegetables and the toothpaste. "It looks good," she said happily.

It didn't. It looked terrible. But Emma didn't say anything. She started flipping through magazine pages again, looking for houses and dogs. She was dying to get a dog, a sweet little puppy with floppy ears, a puppy that she could walk and feed and play fetch with. But no pets were allowed in their apartment. No pets were allowed in the whole big housing project.

That was why Emma wanted to live in a house. She could hardly wait to get a dog. And if they lived in a house, she could have her own bedroom too. She wouldn't have to share with messy Janie anymore.

Emma's parents said houses cost a lot of money. They were saving up to buy one. But it was taking them a long time. Emma wished they would hurry. She turned another page in her magazine.

"Here," said Janie. She held something out.

"What?" Emma looked up.

"It's a house," said Janie. "I found it for you."

Emma took the page. It was a picture of a big white house with a porch, just the kind of house she wanted most. "Thank you," she said. She started to cut the picture around the edges. Sometimes Janie wasn't *so* bad.

"Listen, Janie," she said, "when we move, and I get a dog, I'll let you pet it. Okay?"

"Okay," said Janie.

≫ 2 ≪

Emma and Janie had just put their scrap-books away. It was almost time for dinner. Emma pushed the kitchen window up. She pressed her nose against the screen. It was still raining, but not as hard.

There were puddles in the grass outside and more puddles on the sidewalk. On the other side of the street, people hurried in and out of stores. "If it stops raining, can we go out?" Emma asked.

Her mother was chopping celery for tuna-fish salad. "Maybe after dinner. We'll see." She kept chopping.

Emma sighed. She could hear the television in the living room. Janie and Nick were watching some dumb show. Emma was tired of television. She was tired of being hot and sticky. She turned back to the window.

And then she saw him. He ran across the sidewalk and under the low chain-link fence, onto the grass. He stopped to shake the rain off himself. Then he started running again—right toward Emma.

"He's coming," she yelled. "He's coming."

"Who's coming?" said her mother.

Janie ran into the kitchen. "Who's coming? Daddy?"

"No," said Emma. "The cat."

"Oh." Janie ran over to stand next to Emma at the window.

"Me too, me too," sang Nick as he came into the kitchen. "Pick me up."

Nick was too little to see over the window ledge. He pushed between Emma and Janie.

"Hey," said Janie, "you wet your pants, Nick. You didn't use the potty."

"P-U," said Emma. "That's not all he did. Go away, Nick. You stink."

"No," said Nick. "Pick me up."

Mrs. Tucker scooped Nick up with one arm. She held a small dish in her other hand. "Here, girls. Here's some tuna fish for the cat. Just open the screen a little and put the dish on the ledge. And don't let him in. I'm going to change Nick."

"No," screamed Nick. "No, no, *no.*" He yelled all the way down the hall.

"Here, kitty," said Emma.

"Here, kitty, kitty," said Janie.

The cat jumped up to the window ledge.

"Look, kitty," said Emma. "See what we've got for you." She opened the screen and put the dish outside.

"He's hungry," said Janie. "Look."

"I know," said Emma. "He didn't come yesterday. I wonder where he was." The cat had started coming to their window a few weeks ago, but he didn't come every day. Emma wished he would. He was almost as good as a dog. He would probably make a great pet.

The cat ate and ate. He didn't stop until

he had finished all of the tuna. Then he
shook himself hard. Little drops of rain flew
off him.

"Poor thing," said Emma. "He's all wet.
Maybe we should let him in—just for a
minute."

"No," said Janie. "We'll get in trouble."

Emma reached for the screen. She really
wanted to let the cat in. She wanted to pet
him and . . .

The front door banged shut. "Where is
everybody? I'm home."

"It's Daddy!" cried Emma.

The cat jumped down. Emma watched
him run across the grass.

Mr. Tucker came into the kitchen. "I
need something *cold* to drink," he said.
"Where's your mother? What's for dinner?"

"Tuna fish," said Janie.

"Cat food," said Emma. She giggled.

Mr. Tucker pulled a container of iced tea
out of the refrigerator. *"What?"*

"Daddy," said Emma. "When we get a
house, can we have a dog *and* a cat?"

≫ 3 ≪

Emma scraped the last bit of ice cream from the bottom of her bowl. She wished she could have more, but she knew her mother didn't believe in seconds on dessert.

"Can I go out now, Mommy?" she asked. "It's not raining."

"Me too," said Janie.

Mrs. Tucker pushed back her chair. "I'm going to lie down for a little while, girls. You'll have to ask Daddy."

Emma was surprised. Her mother had never done this before. "Are you sick, Mommy?" she asked.

"No, no. Don't worry, Emma. I'm not sick. I just need a little rest. Be good for Daddy, okay?"

"Okay," said Emma. She watched her mother leave the kitchen.

"Mommy," said Nick. He started to climb out of his high chair.

"Mommy's gone to lie down for a while, Nick," said his father. "How about a little more ice cream?"

"Daddy, can—?" Emma started.

"Just Nick," said her father.

"That's not fair," said Emma.

"No fair, no fair," Janie joined in.

"Oh, all right," said Mr. Tucker. "But just a little." He gave Nick some ice cream. Then he put a tiny scoop in Emma's and Janie's bowls. "That's the end of it anyway," he said. He threw the empty carton into the garbage can.

Emma ate her ice cream in two bites. "Can we go out now, Daddy?"

"Well, I don't know," said her father.

"Please," begged Emma. "It's so hot in here."

Mr. Tucker stood up. "I'll tell you what, girls. If you two will watch Nick while I clean up the kitchen, then you can go out."

Nick was already climbing out of his high chair. "Mommy," he said.

"Come on, Nick. Let's watch television. Mommy's sleeping." Emma tried to steer Nick toward the living room.

But Nick paid no attention. He turned and headed down the hall that led to the bathroom, the linen closet, and the bedrooms. Emma and Janie ran after him. Emma caught him as he was passing the bathroom door.

"Hey, Nick," she said, "you want to go to the potty?"

Nick never wanted to go to the potty. *"No,"* he said. He pulled away from Emma. *"Mommy."*

"Shhhh," said Emma. She grabbed him again. "Mommy is sleeping."

Nick tried to get away.

"Janie, *think* of something." Emma had Nick by the arm. He opened his mouth wide, ready to scream.

"I know," said Janie. "We can let him play in our room."

Nick closed his mouth.

"Are you *crazy?*" said Emma. "He can't play in there. He'll wreck everything." But

15

it was too late. And Emma knew it. If she didn't let him into their room now, Nick would really have a fit. She opened the bedroom door. "Okay, Nick," she said. "You can go in. But you have to be good."

Nick ran into the room. Janie followed him.

Emma pushed past Janie. "If he breaks any of my stuff, I'm going to kill you."

"Don't worry," said Janie. But she looked worried herself.

Nick climbed up on Janie's bed. He picked up her old bear, Mr. Fuzzy.

"Good," said Emma. Now if only Nick would stay on Janie's bed . . .

Nick threw Mr. Fuzzy across the room. Then he climbed down from the bed and ran over to the shelves where Emma and Janie kept their toys and books. He sat down on the floor.

That was all right with Emma. The two bottom shelves were Janie's. Emma had the two top ones.

Nick started pulling Janie's things from the shelves.

"Help me," Janie said to Emma.

"Why?" Emma answered. "This was your idea." But she looked around for something to give Nick. She saw an old coloring book, one she didn't want anymore.

"Janie," she said. "I'll let Nick use my coloring book if you'll let him use your crayons."

"Okay," said Janie. "They're on my little table."

Janie was trying to put her things back as fast as Nick pulled them down. Nick was faster.

Emma went over to the little table. It was covered with Janie's junk. What a slob, thought Emma. Janie never put anything away.

The crayons were scattered around, but Emma found four. She opened the coloring book to an almost clean page. "Look, Nick. Look what I've got for you." She tried to make her voice sound excited, as if she had something great.

Nick looked, but he didn't stand up.

"Come on, Nick. Hurry. You can use *my* coloring book. Won't that be fun?"

"And *my* crayons," said Janie. "But you have to be careful not to break them."

"Are you kidding?" said Emma. "They're already broken. And you did it yourself."

Janie pretended not to hear Emma. She walked over to the little table. "You have to be a *big* boy to use my crayons, Nick. Okay?"

"Okay," said Nick. He stood up and walked over to Emma.

She pulled out the little chair that matched the table.

Nick sat down and picked up a blue crayon.

"You know, Janie . . ." said Emma, "you really should give this table and chair to Nick. You're too big for them."

"I am not," said Janie. "I like them and I'm keeping them for as long as I want."

Emma looked around the room. "It's a big mess in here with your junk all over the place," she said. "There's no room for anything."

"I don't care," said Janie. "You're not the boss."

"Well, when we get a house, I'm not even going to let you into my room—or Nick either."

Nick stopped coloring when he heard his name. He started to get up.

"Wow, Nick, that's great. Look at that coloring." Emma talked fast. She handed Nick a yellow crayon. "You didn't use this one yet," she said.

Nick took the crayon. He made a mark with it. "Pretty." He made another mark. This one was on the table.

"Yes, very pretty," said Emma. She didn't care if he colored on Janie's table, or her little chair either. She wished her father would hurry up. She couldn't wait to go outside. Maybe Carmen would be there.

Carmen Perez lived in the building on the other side of the parking lot in front of Emma's building. She was Emma's best friend.

"I'm going to see if Daddy's almost ready," Emma told Janie. "You watch Nick."

Emma ran down the hall and into the

kitchen. "Daddy," she cried, "are you done yet? Can we go out now?"

Mr. Tucker handed a wet sponge to Emma. "Wipe the table while I finish drying the dishes. Then you can go."

Emma started wiping the table. It felt funny to be working in the kitchen without her mother. She *must* be sick, thought Emma. But then why didn't she say so?

"Finished," said her father. He hung the dish towel up. "You and Janie can go out now."

Emma left the sponge on the table. She ran out of the kitchen and down the hall into her room. She stopped short.

Janie was sitting on the floor with her back to Nick. She was putting her stuffed animals in a neat row on one of her shelves. Nick was coloring with a red crayon—all over the wall.

"Nick!" screamed Emma.

Nick dropped the crayon. He started to cry.

"Janie, you are so *dumb,*" Emma yelled. "Why did you let him do that?"

The wall was a mess—a big, ugly, horrible mess. Just like the rest of the room, thought Emma.

"It's your fault too, Emma," cried Janie.

Nick began crying louder now and stamping his feet.

"Shut up!" Emma yelled at him. "Look what you did to my wall. You're a *bad* boy."

"Mommy, Mommy!" screamed Nick.

Mr. Tucker came running to the door. "What in the world is going on in here?"

Emma and Janie started talking at the same time. "Mommy," Nick sobbed. "I want Mommy."

"I'm here," said Mrs. Tucker from the hallway.

Nick ran over and grabbed her leg.

She picked him up. Then she looked at Emma and Janie. "I think you two should go outside now," she said in a quiet voice. "I'll talk with you later."

≫ 4 ≪

It was hot outside, but there was a little breeze. Emma and Janie stood on the steps in front of their building. Lots of other kids were out too. The sidewalk between the building and the parking lot was crowded.

"I see Richie and Keesha," said Janie. She pointed. "See? Over there by the fence."

"Big deal," said Emma. "Who wants to play with those babies?"

But Janie didn't hear her. She was already running over to join them.

"Don't step in any puddles," Emma called after her. But she knew Janie probably wouldn't listen. Well, too bad for Janie if she got in more trouble.

And Emma knew that they *were* in trouble. She remembered the way her mother had said, "I'll talk with you later." She wished her mother had yelled right away. It was worse when you had to wait. At least it was worse for Emma. Janie didn't seem to mind at all.

"Emma . . . Em-ma . . ." Carmen Perez was calling her from the other side of the parking lot. She had a baby carriage with her. That meant she was baby-sitting Felicia. "Come on over," she called.

"Okay," Emma yelled back. "I just have to tell my sister." She ran over to where Janie was playing with Richie and Keesha. They were pushing pieces of cardboard around in a big puddle.

"We're making boats," Janie told Emma.

"You're making a *mess,*" said Emma. "I'm going over to play with Carmen."

Janie didn't answer. She was busy trying to save a sinking boat.

Emma started to walk around the parking lot. She had to jump out of the way of some big kids zooming by on skateboards.

One of them was Carmen's brother Miguel. He laughed when he saw her jump.

Emma stuck her tongue out at him when she was sure he couldn't see her. She was afraid of him. He was a bully, and his friends were mean too.

Poor Carmen, thought Emma. How could she live with that Miguel? And she had a little brother named Hector who was a real pain too. Just like Nick. Miguel and Hector shared a bedroom.

Carmen shared *her* room with her new baby sister. Emma thought Felicia was the most beautiful baby she had ever seen. She was like a doll—a doll that moved and could really drink from a bottle. It would be fun to share a room with her.

Emma walked faster. The sidewalk had lots of puddles. Mothers screamed at little kids to stay out of them. A group of older kids was playing hide-and-seek. Teenagers sat on cars in the parking lot with their radios playing. It seemed as if there were people everywhere.

"Emma," called Carmen, "I've got Felicia."

"I know," said Emma, when she reached the carriage. She bent over and looked in at the baby. "Ooooo," she said, "she's so cute."

"She's not *that* great," said Carmen. "You should hear her scream in the middle of the night."

But Emma knew that Carmen really loved Felicia. She could tell by the way Carmen looked at the baby.

"Oh, I wish I had a little baby like this, instead of that dumb Nick," said Emma.

Felicia had soft little curls on her head. Her brown eyes were open. She looked up at Emma. Emma reached out and touched one of the baby's tiny gold earrings. Felicia waved a small fist in the air.

"Does your mother let you give her a bath yet?" Emma asked.

"She lets me help," said Carmen proudly. "And today she let me pick out her clothes and help dress her."

Felicia was wearing a pink sunsuit. And little white socks with pink trim.

"Oh, you're so lucky," said Emma. "Can I push the carriage?"

"Okay," said Carmen, "if you're careful."

Emma and Carmen walked back and forth in front of Carmen's building. People stopped to look into the carriage at Felicia. Everybody smiled and said what a beautiful baby she was.

"If I had a baby sister," Emma told Carmen, "we could push the carriages together. We could pretend that we were mothers."

"That would be fun," Carmen agreed, "but I'll share Felicia with you."

"I know," said Emma. "But it's not the same." She wanted to have a baby at home, just like Carmen. She wanted to feed her and give her a bath and dress her up. When Nick was born, Emma had been too young to do those things. But now she was old enough.

"If you come up to my apartment, you

can hold Felicia," said Carmen. "I know my mother will let you."

"Really?" Emma was dying to hold the baby. "Can I come tomorrow? My mother's mad at me, so I can't ask her now."

"No, not tomorrow. We're going to my aunt's house. How come your mother is mad at you?"

"It's not my fault," said Emma. "I'm always getting in trouble because of Janie and Nick."

Just then Janie ran up. "It's time to go in," she said. "Mommy's calling us."

Emma got a funny feeling in her stomach. She didn't want to go in. She didn't want to hear what her mother was going to say.

"I've got to go," she said to Carmen.

"Okay," said Carmen. "Maybe I'll see you tomorrow after we get home."

Janie had already started back. Emma hurried to catch up with her. "Do you think she's still mad?" asked Emma.

Janie was jumping over puddles. "Who?"

"Mommy. Don't you remember about Nick coloring on the—"

"*Emma, Janie* . . . time to come in."

"We're coming," yelled Janie, and she started to run.

The apartment felt even hotter than before. Emma wanted to run right back outside.

"Time to wash up and brush your teeth, girls," said Mrs. Tucker. "Nick is already in bed."

"Do we have to go to bed so early?" asked Emma. Maybe this would be their punishment.

"No," said her mother, "but Daddy and I want to talk to you when you're cleaned up."

That was what Emma was afraid of. Janie seemed a little nervous now too. She didn't fool around in the bathroom at all. She and Emma washed up and brushed their teeth quietly.

When they were both ready, they went into the living room.

Their mother and father were sitting on the couch. Emma and Janie sat on chairs.

"Girls," said their mother.

"We're sorry," Emma burst out. "And we won't ever do it again."

"Do *what?*" said her mother.

"The crayon . . ." Emma began.

Her mother and father looked at each other. "Don't worry about the crayon," said her mother. "There's something else we want to tell both of you."

"We weren't going to say anything yet," said their father, "because it's not going to happen for a long time, but . . . But your mother isn't feeling too well, and we thought you might worry, so . . ."

All of a sudden Emma felt frozen inside. Her mother *was* sick. That was what was wrong. Maybe she would even have to go to the hospital. Maybe she would even . . .

Emma started to cry. She couldn't help it. Janie began crying too.

"Girls, what's the matter? Why are you crying?"

Emma ran over and threw herself on her

mother. "Mommy, Mommy," she cried, "I don't want you to die." She held on to her as tight as she could.

"Emma, listen to me. I'm not going to die. I'm not sick. I'm just going to have a baby."

Emma pulled away from her mother. She stared at her.

"A *baby?*" she said.

≫ 5 ≪

A baby! Emma couldn't believe it. How wonderful! She wiped her tears away.

"Oh, Mommy," she cried. "Now we'll have a tiny baby, just like Carmen's. I can't wait."

Her mother smiled. "I'm glad you're happy about it, Emma," she said. She gave her a hug.

"Me too," said Janie. "I want a baby too, but only if it's a girl. I don't like Nick."

"Of course you like Nick," said her mother.

"No, we don't," said Emma. "All he ever does is yell and scream and make a mess." Emma remembered the red crayon marks on her bedroom wall.

"Listen," said their father, "you two

weren't exactly perfect when you were Nick's age, you know."

"But we weren't as bad as Nick," said Janie.

Emma thought Janie probably had been as bad as Nick, but she didn't say so. She wanted to talk about the new baby, not dumb old Nick.

"When is the baby coming?" she asked. "Can I give her a bath and dress her and—"

"Hold on," said her mother. "The baby is not coming for a long time. Almost six months. And it might be a *him.*"

"I know," said Emma. "But can I give it a bath? *Pleeeease?* Mrs. Perez lets Carmen help with Felicia's bath, and . . . You know, maybe we can name *our* baby Felicia too."

"No," said Janie. "Sarah." Sarah was Janie's best friend from school.

"How about Daniel or Matthew or Max?" said Mr. Tucker. "Those are nice names."

"Those are *boys'* names," said Emma. "We don't want a boy."

"Listen, girls," said their mother, "we have lots of time to think about names. But right now it's about time for you to go to bed."

"No, no," said Janie. "It's too early."

"It's too *hot,*" said Emma. "I can't sleep when it's so hot."

"I'll tell you what," said their mother. "You can sleep in just your underwear tonight. It *is* awfully warm."

"But Mommy—" began Emma.

"No *buts.* Bedtime. Go on into your room. I'll be in soon for your story."

Emma and Janie walked slowly out of the living room and down the hall to their bedroom.

Emma sat on the edge of her bed. It would be fun to have her own baby sister's crib in the room, she thought. Just like Carmen.

She looked around the room. Where would it fit? The room was really crowded. There were the two beds and the big dresser and Janie's table and chair set and the shelves and . . .

There wasn't any space to put a crib.

If only Janie didn't have so much stuff, thought Emma. She really should give her table and chair to Nick. There must be a way. . . .

And then Emma had a great idea. She watched Janie struggling to take her shirt off. "I'll help you with your shirt," she said in a friendly voice.

Janie looked surprised. "You will?" she said.

"Sure I will." Emma tried to smile a big-sister smile.

"Why?" said Janie. "What do you want?"

Emma smiled harder. "Nothing," she said. "Come here. I'll help you, and then I'll tell you about this great idea I have."

Janie finished taking her shirt off by herself. "What idea?"

She doesn't trust me, thought Emma. "Well, you see," she said, "I was thinking that there isn't enough room in here for a crib."

"That's okay," said Janie. "The baby can sleep in Nick's room."

"No she *can't,*" said Emma. "She needs to be in here with me, so I can take care of her." She rushed on before Janie could interrupt. "And I was thinking that if *you* moved into Nick's room, you could share your little table with him, but it would still be *your* table, and there'd be plenty of room in here for—"

"*No,*" said Janie.

"It would only be for a little while," said Emma quickly. "Until we move. Then we'll all have our own rooms."

Janie sat on her bed. "*You* can share with Nick. I'll share with the baby." She pulled her sandals off. "I can take care of her."

"No you can't," said Emma. "You're not old enough."

"Well, I'm not sharing with Nick—and you can't make me."

Emma didn't say anything. Maybe she could talk to her mother about this later, when Janie wasn't around. Her mother would understand.

Mrs. Tucker came into the room. "Whose bed do I sit on tonight?" she asked.

"It's my turn," said Emma. "Last night you sat on Janie's."

"All right." Her mother sat down and opened the book of folktales.

Emma tried to listen to the story, but she couldn't stop thinking about the baby. She hoped her mother would let her feed the baby and dress it and give it a bath.

But most of all, she hoped the baby would be a girl. Emma would think of a way to get Janie out of the room. Then she could share with the baby. It would be so much fun. She could pick her up and hold her whenever she wanted.

Maybe she would even keep the baby in her room when they moved to a house. Just until she was big enough for her own room.

Emma closed her eyes. She could see the new house in her mind. Her room would be blue and white, with a canopy bed and a desk of her own and her puppy's basket.

The baby's room would be yellow, with . . .

"The end," said Mrs. Tucker. She closed the book. "That was a pretty good story, wasn't it?"

"Can we hear another one?" Janie asked. "That one was too short."

"Tomorrow," said her mother. "Now it's time to go to—"

"Mommy," said Emma. "It's a good thing we didn't move yet. You know why?"

"Why?"

"Because now we need a bigger house. So the baby can have her own room."

"Emma—" said her mother.

"I know she won't need a room right away," Emma went on. "She can stay with me until she's about a year old. And then—"

"Emma, listen. We haven't talked about this yet, but . . . we're not going to look for a house for a while."

"Why?" said Emma. "For how long?" She didn't like the way her mother was looking at her, kind of serious and sad.

"Daddy and I want a house as much as

39

you do. You know we do. But having a baby costs a lot of money. It's going to take a couple of years to—"

"Years!" cried Emma. "Years!" She couldn't believe it. Her beautiful bedroom, her little puppy . . .

"I don't want to move," said Janie. "I want to stay here with my friends."

"Well, *I* don't want to stay here and share a room with *you,*" said Emma. "It's not fair." She felt tears stinging her eyes. She wanted the new baby, but . . .

"You know, Emma," said her mother. "You would miss Carmen if we moved, and your other friends too."

"I know," said Emma. "But you said Carmen could visit me. And if we don't move, I can't have my own room, and we can't get a puppy, and I wanted to share a room with the baby, and there's no place to put anything in here."

"We'll think of something," said her mother. "We can't get a house, but there must be something we can do." She looked around the room.

"I won't share a room with Nick," said Janie. "I *won't.*"

"Nobody said you had to," said her mother.

"*See.*" Janie stuck her tongue out at Emma. "I told you so."

"Girls." Mrs. Tucker stood up. "I said we'll think of something. But not tonight. It's late, and we're all tired."

"I'm not tired," said Emma and Janie together.

"Well, *I* am," said their mother. She kissed them both. Then she turned off the light. "Be good. Go to sleep. See you in the morning."

Emma could hear her footsteps going down the hall.

"Janie," she said quietly, "if you'll share Nick's room, I'll give you something very, very special."

"No," said Janie. "But what is it?"

"I'm not telling. It's a secret." Emma wondered what she could give Janie. She couldn't think of a thing.

"You're just making it up," said Janie. "You can't fool me."

"Quiet back there," called their father. "Not another word."

"Okay," Emma called back. She didn't want to talk to Janie anyway. She wanted to be quiet. She had a lot of thinking to do.

≫ 6 ≪

Janie was sucking her thumb. She did that when she was sleeping. Emma wished that she could fall asleep too. But she couldn't stop thinking.

Everything was jumbled up in her head. The baby, her bedroom, Janie, the new house, her puppy.

And she was so hot.

Emma flipped over onto her stomach. That didn't help. She turned back again. If only she could get cooler. Her pillowcase was hot and damp. So were the sheets. She would *never* fall asleep.

Emma sat up and swung her feet over the edge of her bed. It must be very late, she thought. She listened. Outside it was quiet except for a passing car. Someone yelled, but it sounded far away. Then it was quiet again.

In the room, Emma could hear the little noises Janie made when she sucked her thumb. Down the hall, the television buzzed faintly from the living room.

Emma stood up. She tiptoed carefully out of her room and down the hallway. She stopped in the entrance to the living room.

"Emma!" said her mother. "What are you doing up? You should have been asleep a long time ago."

"But I *can't,*" said Emma. She walked over to the couch where her mother and father were sitting. "I tried and tried, but I'm too hot, and my head won't stop thinking about things."

"You mean about the baby?" said her mother gently.

"Yes," said Emma. "And other things too. And I really can't go to sleep."

"I have an idea," said Mr. Tucker.

"What?" asked Emma.

"Well," he said, "I was just going to go

out to get some ice cream. Maybe you'd like to come along."

"Oh, I *would,*" cried Emma.

Her mother smiled. "Go get your clothes. Bring them out here, so you don't wake Janie up."

Emma ran back to her bedroom. Her bare feet made almost no sound. She scooped up her shorts and T-shirt and sandals.

By the light from the hall, she could see that Janie was still asleep. Poor Janie. She would be sad if she knew what she was missing. Emma felt sorry for her, but she was still glad Janie wasn't coming. This was going to be an extra-special treat, and Emma didn't want to share it.

She ran back to the living room. "I'm ready," she said, pulling her clothes on. She could hardly believe she was going out with her father alone—no Janie, no Nick. Emma hugged herself and did a happy little dance.

"Well, let's go." Her father was waiting. "I'm ready too."

"Have a nice walk," said Mrs. Tucker. "Don't forget to bring me back some ice cream."

Emma unlocked the door to the hallway. She pulled it open. "Bye, Mommy," she called. "We won't forget."

It was very quiet in the hall. Not at all like the daytime. No people talking, no radios, no doors slamming. And the lights seemed different—more yellow. It felt spooky.

Emma took her father's hand. They walked past apartment 1-A, past the elevator, and into the lobby. Her father opened the big front door.

It was cooler outside, and very dark. They stood on the steps for a minute.

Hardly anyone else was out. Emma looked around. Some men were in the parking lot. It was too dark to see them clearly, but she could hear them talking in low voices. Emma was glad she wasn't alone. She looked up at her father.

"Take a deep breath, Emma," he said. "What do you smell?"

Emma was surprised, but she did it. "It's nice," she said. "It smells cool and—different. Not like cars and stuff."

"I like the way it smells at night too," said her father quietly. He took another deep breath. "I guess we'd better get going." They started to walk.

"Are we going to the grocery store?" asked Emma.

"It's been closed for hours." Her father led her past the small group in the parking lot. "We'll go to the candy store on the next block. It stays open very late."

"Okay," said Emma. She looked up at her father. He was so tall and strong. She felt proud to be with him. She didn't care where they went. It was wonderful just being out with him alone.

They were at the end of the parking lot now, where it opened out to the street. Emma could see that the stores on the other side of the street were closed. Most of them had metal gates pulled across their fronts.

She looked back at her own building. "Daddy," she said. "I can see our kitchen window." She pointed.

"Yes, that's it," said her father.

As they walked, Emma ran her hand along the short chain fence that separated the sidewalk from the grassy place around her building. She remembered the cat running across the wet grass. It seemed so long ago. Not like the very same day.

She looked at her bedroom window. It was dark. It had an empty look. But she knew that Janie was sleeping inside. Probably still sucking her thumb. Nick was asleep in his bedroom across the hall. And her mother was watching television in the living room, waiting for Emma to come home.

Emma felt safe and warm and happy. She was going out into the night, but her father was there to protect her, and the rest of her family would be waiting for her when she came back home.

"Daddy," said Emma. "Would you miss our apartment if we moved away?"

"Ummm," said her father. He thought for a moment. "I'd miss some of the people we know, and some other things too, but not the apartment. It's too crowded."

"Me too," said Emma. She knew just how her father felt. "And it's going to be *more* crowded when the baby comes. Right?"

"Well, yes. But we'll be okay. We'll just make room for the baby."

"Daddy, do you think I'm old enough to take care of her—the baby? I mean give her a bath and dress her?"

"I'm not sure, Emma."

They came to the corner. The light was red. It seemed a brighter red than it did in the daytime. They stopped even though no cars were coming. "But Daddy," said Emma, "Carmen's mother lets *her* help with Felicia."

"Every family is different," said Mr. Tucker. The light turned green. He stepped off the curb. "If you want to help with the new baby, you have to show us that you're old enough, that you're responsible."

"How?" asked Emma.

"By doing things for your mother, like helping her watch Nick and being nice to Janie and . . ."

"Yuck," said Emma.

Her father laughed. "You asked me," he said. "And that's my answer."

That was *not* the answer Emma wanted. Helping with Nick was no fun, and being nice to Janie was impossible.

Emma thought about giving the new baby a bath. She thought about dressing her and taking her for walks in the carriage with Carmen. Janie wouldn't be old enough to do those things, but Emma knew that *she* was old enough. She would just have to prove it. "I can be responsible," she said.

"Good," said her father.

"Daddy . . ."

"Here we are."

Emma followed her father into the candy store. The bright lights made her blink. It was crowded, but she couldn't see any other kids. She was the only one out so late.

Emma felt special, but a little nervous too. She stayed close to her father.

"I want vanilla, Daddy," she said quietly. "Please."

Her father ordered two vanilla cones when it was his turn. And one cup of chocolate to take back for Mrs. Tucker.

Emma was glad to get out of the store. She took a little bite of her ice cream.

They had to walk quickly so the chocolate wouldn't melt before they got home. Emma's ice cream was melting too. She nibbled at the cone and licked around the edges.

"Daddy . . ." she said between licks, "I really wanted to move, and now Mommy says we can't."

"I know you did, Emma. We all wanted to have a house. And we *will*. We just have to wait."

Emma didn't want to wait. She licked a drop of ice cream from her hand. She almost had to run to keep up with her father.

"Daddy," she said. Maybe she should ask him about sharing a room with the baby.

"We're home," said Mr. Tucker. He ran up the front steps and opened the door for Emma. "Let's hurry before there's nothing left for your mother."

Emma ran after him.

"Daddy . . ." she tried again. If she didn't talk to him now, she might never have another chance. She couldn't ask him while her mother was there, or Janie.

Her father was unlocking the apartment door. "Yes, Emma?" He pushed the door open.

It was too late. "Nothing. . . . I mean, thank you for the ice cream." She popped the last bite of cone into her mouth.

"Did you remember me?" called Mrs. Tucker from the living room.

"We got you chocolate." Emma brought the ice cream to her mother.

"Mmmmm . . . my favorite." Her mother got up from the couch. "Emma, it's really terribly late. I want you to get right to bed."

"But what if I still can't sleep?" said Emma. "I might stay awake all night."

"*Emma,*" said her father. And Emma could tell from the way he said it that he meant business.

"Okay," she said. She didn't want her father to be angry at her now. It would spoil the special time they had just had together. Emma kissed her parents and started off down the hall to her bedroom.

She would just have to find another time to be alone with him. Emma crawled into her bed. She yawned. She would just have to. . . .

≫ 7 ≪

When Emma woke up the next morning, sunshine filled her room. She could hear Janie and Nick at the other end of the apartment. But Emma didn't want to get up yet. She wanted to think about last night.

She remembered how dark and quiet it had been outside, and how she and her father had stood on the front steps smelling the night air. And she remembered what her father had said about the baby. If Emma wanted to take care of her, she would have to show her parents that she was old enough. It was going to be hard.

Just then, Janie raced into the room. "Get up, Emma," she yelled. "Mommy wants you to get up right now."

"Go away," said Emma.

Janie stuck her tongue out. "Make me,"

she said. "Anyway, we're going grocery shopping, and Mommy says you have to come."

Emma groaned.

It was crowded in the supermarket. Mrs. Tucker pushed the shopping cart, Nick rode in the baby seat, and Emma and Janie walked alongside.

"Can I push the cart?" said Emma. "I'm big enough."

"You can try," said her mother. She let go of the cart and went over to get a box of cookies from a high shelf.

Janie went with her.

Emma felt very grown-up. "I'm going to push you," she said to Nick. She grabbed the handle of the cart.

"No," said Nick. "I want Mommy."

Emma pushed.

"No!" yelled Nick. Then he kicked her, right on her chin.

"Ow!" cried Emma. She slapped Nick's leg as hard as she could.

Nick screamed. Everybody turned to look.

Mrs. Tucker ran over. "What happened?"

"Nick kicked me," said Emma. "Right here." She had to yell because Nick was still screaming.

"If Nick kicked *you*," Mrs. Tucker yelled back, "then why is *Nick* crying?"

"I hit him back a little," said Emma.

"Emma hit me. She hit me," cried Nick. He pointed to the red mark on his leg where Emma had slapped him.

"Oh, Emma," said her mother. "How could you? Nick's just a baby. He didn't mean to kick you."

Emma couldn't believe her ears. Her mother hadn't even seen what happened. Of *course* Nick meant to kick her.

"He did so," said Emma. "He did it on purpose. And it hurt." She put her hand on her chin.

Mrs. Tucker just shook her head. Then she opened the box of cookies and gave one to Nick.

Nick stopped crying and stuffed the cookie into his mouth.

The little brat, thought Emma. She made a terrible face at him.

"Emma, that's enough," said her mother. "Act your age."

Emma hated it when anyone said that to her. She walked behind as her mother pushed the cart. She didn't want to help anymore. Why did her mother blame her for everything? It just wasn't fair.

Mrs. Tucker stopped walking. "Emma," she said. "You and Janie can help by getting things for me." She looked at her grocery list. "We need cereal. You can start with that."

"Can we pick whatever we want?" asked Janie.

"Cornflakes," said her mother. "The kind we always get."

Emma knew what kind that was—the cheap kind. Her mother was always trying to save money.

Janie started off by herself. "Come on, Emma."

Emma dragged her feet. Dumb cornflakes,

she thought. Dumb Janie and Nick. Dumb mother.

Up and down the aisles they went. Emma and Janie found cornflakes, peanut butter, tuna fish, milk, and canned peas. They brought everything back to the cart.

"You really were a big help, girls," said their mother at the checkout counter. She smiled at them.

But Emma refused to smile back. She was still angry.

≫ 8 ≪

Outside, the sun beat down on their heads. "I've got the groceries, girls. You take care of Nick."

"Okay," said Janie. She took one of Nick's hands. Emma took the other.

"No!" said Nick.

"Yes," said Emma, and she held his hand tighter.

Nick tried to pull away. Then he tried to kick Emma.

"See?" said Emma. "See what Nick is doing?"

"I'm losing my patience, Emma. Let go of his hand. Just see that he stays on the sidewalk."

Emma dropped Nick's hand. So did Janie.

Nick started to run.

"Nick," called Mrs. Tucker. "Stop running—right now."

Nick stopped.

"I'm hot," Janie whined.

"We're almost home," said her mother. "I'll make some lemonade."

Emma loved lemonade. She wished they were home already. The sidewalk was burning her feet right through her sandals. Sweat was trickling down her back. Her hair stuck to her neck.

Nick started running again. "Water," he cried. "I see water."

Emma and Janie ran after him.

And then Emma saw it too. Someone had opened a fire hydrant at the end of the block. A wonderful spray of water was shooting out, and kids were running through it screaming and laughing.

"Emma," said Janie, "maybe Mommy will let us."

"She won't," said Emma. "She never does."

But Janie wasn't listening. She ran back to her mother. "Mommy," she yelled as she ran, "can we . . ."

Mrs. Tucker caught up with Emma and Nick. "It's too dangerous," she was saying to Janie. "Cars are going by, and some of those big kids could push you down, and there might be glass in the street."

"We'd be careful, Mommy. . . . Please," Janie begged.

Nick just yelled, "Water!" over and over again. He jumped up and down in place.

Emma kept walking. She was closer to the hydrant now. She could even feel a few drops of cold water against her skin. She stopped. She was dying to run through the spray, to be cold and wet and . . .

All of a sudden, a big kid dashed out of the spray. He ran over to Emma, picked her up, and ran back into the water.

"Miguel Perez!" Emma screamed. "Put me *down.*" The water felt like icy needles. She tried to get away.

Miguel laughed. "What's the matter? You afraid of a little water?" He put her back

in the same spot. Water dripped from her
hair down her face. Her shirt and shorts
had big wet spots.

Her mother was waiting. "Miguel," she
said. She sounded angry.

"Uh, hello, Mrs. Tucker. It's so hot, I
didn't think a little water would hurt."

"Me too, me too." Nick grabbed Miguel's
hand.

"It's okay," said Miguel. "Look, my
friends and me, we're taking turns watching
for cars."

Nick pulled Miguel's hand.

"Oh, all right," said Mrs. Tucker. "But
please be careful."

Miguel picked up Nick. He ran into the
water.

Now Janie was jumping up and down.
"Mommy, can—"

"Go ahead," said her mother. "Both of
you."

Emma ran right into the spray. Janie
hung back. She stuck her hands in, and
then her feet.

"Come on in," Emma called to her.

"Don't be a chicken." She dashed out of the water, took Janie's hand, and pulled. Janie shrieked, but Emma pulled harder until Janie was in the spray.

Soon they were both soaking wet. "Look what I can do," said Emma. She held her nose and let the water hit her face.

"I can do it too," Janie yelled. "And I can do another trick. Watch me." She turned round and round in the spray.

That looked like fun, so Emma tried it too. She was having a wonderful time. "Isn't this great?" she said to Janie.

"It's freezing," said Janie. She laughed.

They ran out of the water for a moment.

Miguel came over. He put Nick down next to Emma. "You take him now," he said. Then he ran off to join his friends.

Emma held Nick's hand.

"More," cried Nick.

"Janie, you take his other hand," said Emma. "Let's run with him."

Emma and Nick and Janie ran back into the water. Emma took small steps so that Nick wouldn't fall down.

More and more kids kept coming. It was getting crowded. Emma had to be careful not to let any of the big kids bump into Janie or Nick. Back and forth they ran, through the icy spray, screaming and laughing.

"*Em-ma . . . Janie . . .*" It was their mother. "Time to go."

They had to pull Nick away. Emma and Janie didn't want to leave either.

All three of them were still soaking wet when they got home.

"Go get some dry clothes on, girls," said their mother. She peeled Nick's wet shirt off.

Emma and Janie went back to their room. "That was fun," said Emma. "I hope Mommy lets us do it again."

"Me too," Janie answered. She kicked off her wet sandals. "Can we see it from our window?"

They ran over and pressed their faces against the screen.

"No," said Emma. The hydrant was too far down the block for them to see it. "But look," she cried. "The cat's coming. He's on the grass."

"Here, kitty, kitty," called Janie.

"*Psss, psss, psss,*" said Emma.

The cat stopped. He looked toward their window. Then he walked over and leaped up to the sill.

"Nice kitty," said Janie. "Good kitty."

"He's lonely," said Emma. She ran over and closed the bedroom door. Then she came back to the window. She started to push the screen up.

"What are you doing?" Janie said.

"Shhh," Emma whispered. "I'm going to let him in. Just for a minute."

"But you can't. Mommy—"

"It's okay," Emma said. "She won't find out. Don't you want to pet him?" Emma pushed the screen up a little more. "Here, kitty, kitty," she called softly.

≫ 9 ≪

"Here, kitty," said Emma. *"Psss, psss, psss."* She put her hand out slowly. She didn't want to scare him away.

The cat looked at Emma for a moment, then he jumped past her, down onto the floor. He landed with a small thud and stood there looking around.

"Oooooo, he's in," whispered Janie.

Emma bent down and gently touched his head. "He's really soft," she said. "And he's friendly."

"I want to pet him too." Janie squatted next to Emma. She ran her hand along the cat's back. "He likes me."

"See?" said Emma. "I told you it would be all right." She petted him again.

The cat pushed his head against her hand. He meowed.

Emma pulled her hand away. "Shhh, kitty." She looked nervously at the door.

The cat meowed again—louder. His mouth opened wide.

"Make him go outside," said Janie. "Mommy's going to hear him. And I don't like his teeth."

"Okay," said Emma. "Time to go out now, cat." She pointed to the window so the cat would understand.

The cat did *not* understand. He rubbed against her ankle, his tail held high in the air. *"Meow,"* he cried. *"Meow."*

"Oh, no," said Emma. "I know what's wrong. He's hungry. And we can't get food." Why hadn't she thought of that before she let him in?

The cat meowed again. He ran up to Janie.

Janie backed away. "I don't like him anymore. I'm getting Mommy."

"Don't be dumb," Emma told her. "Do you want to get in trouble for letting him in?"

"*I* didn't let him in. *You* did. I'm telling."

"Meoooow."

Suddenly the bedroom door opened.

Emma and Janie jumped.

Their mother came into the room. She stopped when she saw the cat. She looked angry. "How many times do I have to tell you that—"

"Mommy, he's *hungry*," said Emma.

Her mother picked the cat up. She carried him over to the window and gently put him down outside. She closed the screen. "You can get some food for him in a minute," she said. "But first I want to know who let him in."

"Emma did it," said Janie. "I told her not to."

"Tattletale," said Emma. "*You* didn't have to pet him, you know."

"Janie," said her mother, "go get some of the leftover tuna salad for the cat."

Janie ran out of the room.

Emma gave her a dirty look as she ran past.

"Emma," said her mother. "How many

times do I have to tell you something before you listen?"

"I—" Emma started.

"Look at yourself."

Emma looked down.

"Still in your wet clothes. I've changed Nick and put away the groceries, and what have you done?"

"Janie—"

"I don't want to hear about Janie. *You* let the cat in. And Janie's three years younger than you, anyway."

"But—"

"No *buts,*" said her mother. "No excuses. You say you want to take care of the new baby, and then you behave like this. You slap your little brother and make him cry, and then you let the cat in when you *know* no animals are allowed."

Emma looked at her feet.

"Well," her mother went on, "if this is the way you're going to show me how responsible you are, you can just forget about taking care of a baby. And I mean it." She turned and marched out of the room just as Janie was coming in with the tuna fish.

Janie looked out the window. "The cat's gone," she said. "Maybe he *wasn't* hungry."

"Tattletale," said Emma in a low voice. "You'll be sorry." Then she went to the dresser and got some dry clothes out. She took them over to her bed.

Janie got dressed quickly and raced out of the room. She took the tuna fish with her.

Emma sat on the edge of her bed, her dry clothes next to her. No house, she thought—no blue and white bedroom, no puppy. And now she wouldn't be taking care of the baby either. Emma stared at the red crayon marks on her wall. She started to cry.

Nick came to the door. He stopped when he saw Emma crying and stood there staring at her. Emma almost never cried.

Emma didn't yell at him to get out. She didn't care. She didn't care if he wrecked the whole place.

≫ 10 ≪

Nick waited near the doorway for a minute. Then he walked over and put his hand on Emma's knee. "Don't cry, Emma," he said. He looked very small and sad standing there.

Emma lifted him up and sat him next to her on the bed. "It's okay," she said. "Don't be sad, Nick." But she couldn't stop crying herself. Her throat burned, and her eyes felt swollen.

Nick patted her arm. That made Emma cry harder.

"*Em-ma . . .*" called Mrs. Tucker. "*Nick . . .* time for lunch."

Emma didn't answer. She listened to her mother's footsteps coming down the hall. She looked at herself. She was still in her wet clothes. She hadn't done a single thing since her mother had yelled at her. Now she'd be in even more trouble.

Mrs. Tucker came into the room. She stopped when she saw Emma and Nick. "What happened?" she asked.

Emma didn't say anything.

"Emma crying," said Nick.

"Emma," said her mother, "what's the matter? Are you crying just because I yelled at you?"

Emma shook her head.

"Well, then why?"

"It's . . . it's because of *everything,*" Emma sobbed.

"Oh, Emma," said her mother. She came over and sat next to her. "I'm sorry if I was too rough on you, but you *did* slap Nick, and you *did* let the cat in, and . . ."

"It's not that," said Emma. "It's . . . my puppy."

"Your *puppy?*"

"Now I can't have one," cried Emma. "And I really wanted one so much, and my

own room too." Emma looked around the crowded, messy bedroom. So did her mother.

"And," said Emma, "now I can't even take care of the new baby or *anything.*"

"Emma crying," said Nick again.

"Yes, I know, Nick," said his mother. "You can go play with Janie now. Emma will be all right."

Nick stayed where he was.

"I *won't* be all right." Emma shook her head.

"Yes, you will," said her mother. "It was wrong of me to say that about the baby."

"It was?" Emma sniffed. This was not what she expected to hear.

"Yes," said her mother. "I was hot and tired and . . . and I forgot how you helped Janie and Nick on the way home."

"I did?" said Emma.

"In the water," said her mother. "Remember?"

Emma did remember. "But we were having fun."

Her mother smiled. "Does it have to be so terrible to take care of Nick or be nice to your sister? Is there a rule that it can't ever be fun?"

Emma thought for a moment. It was true. She *had* held their hands, and she *had* protected them from the bigger kids. And it *had* been fun. It really had.

"Mommy," said Emma. "I'm sorry I let the cat in. I won't do it again."

"Good."

"And I'm sorry I slapped Nick so hard. But he kicked me."

"I know, I know," said her mother. She gave Emma a hug. "Let's forget about all that now. Let's go have some lunch. Okay?"

"Okay," said Emma.

"Okay," said Nick. He hopped off the bed and ran across the room.

Emma looked at the back of Nick's shorts. Then she looked at the big wet spot on her bed. Yuck. "Mommy, Nick wet his pants and—"

"It was time to wash your sheets anyway," said her mother. She got up and followed Nick out of the room.

"Hurry up and change your clothes,
Emma," she called back. "Then come for
lunch."

Emma peeled her damp clothes off. She
left them on the bed, next to Nick's wet
spot. Then she got dressed and went to the
kitchen.

"Lemonade and peanut butter sand-
wiches," said Janie, not looking at Emma.

Emma sat down and picked up her lemonade. She finished half the glass.
"Mmmm," she said. "Good."

"Don't drink it so fast," said her mother.
"You'll make yourself sick."

"Okay." Emma took a bite of her sand-
wich. And then another. She was really
hungry. "Janie," she said between bites,
"do you want to work on scrapbooks after
lunch?"

Janie looked at her nervously. "You're
not mad at me anymore?"

"No," said Emma. "It's okay." She remembered what her mother had told her about how it could be fun to be nice to Janie. She smiled at her sister.

"I call beautiful ladies," said Janie. "And cats."

Emma sighed.

"Kitty," said Nick. He pointed to the window.

Emma and Janie jumped up from the table. Janie got the tuna fish from the refrigerator while Emma pushed the kitchen screen up.

"Looks like we'll have to add cat food to the grocery list," said Mrs. Tucker. She smiled at Emma.

Emma smiled back. She knew her mother was trying to make her feel better. "You mean we can feed him all the time?" she asked.

"Yes," said her mother. "But you still have to remember that—"

"I know," said Emma. "He can't come in."

Emma reached under the screen to touch the cat. He rubbed his head against her hand. "Don't worry, kitty," she told him. "We're going to feed you whenever you come here. Real cat food."

Janie pushed the dish out onto the ledge. The cat ate in small gulps.

And, thought Emma, some day when we finally get a house, you can come with us and live indoors, kitty.

Emma was sure the cat would love living in a real house.

She hoped he'd like her dog.

» 11 «

Emma and Janie sat at the kitchen table. Janie was gluing a picture of a beautiful lady into her scrapbook. She hummed as she worked. Glue squished out from the edges when she pressed the picture down.

Yuck, thought Emma. But she didn't say a word. Her mother was putting Nick in for his nap, and Emma and Janie had promised to be quiet.

Emma wished it wasn't so hot. The backs of her legs stuck to the chair. She flipped through the pages of her magazine. So far she hadn't found one good picture. She turned the pages more slowly.

Suddenly she stopped.

"Oh," she said. "Look what I found. It's so cute."

"Let me see," said Janie.

Emma held up the magazine.

"It's a cat," said Janie. "You have to give it to me."

"No," said Emma. "It's not a cat. It's a . . . *kitten*." She pulled the magazine back away from Janie's reach. "And it's mine."

The kitten's fur looked as soft as a cloud, and its mouth was open so you could see its tiny white teeth and pink tongue. Emma loved it.

"It is *too* a cat," said Janie. Her voice was getting louder. "I'm going to tell Mommy."

"Be quiet," said Emma. She was sorry she had said anything about the picture. She should have just cut it out and pasted it in her book. She looked at the kitten again. It was so cute. She just couldn't give it to Janie. She'd only mess it up.

"It's not fair," Janie whined. "And I *am* going to tell."

"Janie," said Emma quickly, "if you let me keep this kitten, I'll find you another good picture, a better one. I promise."

"No," said Janie.

"Please," Emma begged.

"*No.*" Janie got up from her chair. She started toward the hall.

"Wait," called Emma.

Janie stopped.

"Don't tell Mommy. I'll give it to you."

Janie came back. She held out her hand.

"On one condition," said Emma. "You have to let me cut it out and paste it in for you."

Janie got a stubborn look on her face. "I can do it myself."

"Well, that's my condition," said Emma. "Take it or leave it." If she couldn't have the picture for herself, at least she could keep Janie from ruining it.

"I'll tell," said Janie.

"Go ahead. You can scream your head off if you want to." Janie wasn't the only one who could be stubborn.

"Oh, all right," said Janie. She sat down.

Emma picked up her scissors. She cut the picture out as carefully as she could. Then she spread a little bit of glue on the back. "Give me your scrapbook," she said.

Janie handed it over. Then she watched as Emma placed the kitten in the middle of a blank page.

"You can press it down," Emma said. She passed the scrapbook back.

Janie did, gently. Not one drop of glue squished out.

"It looks good," said Emma. "Don't put anything else on that page."

"I can if I want to," said Janie. She looked at the kitten. "Okay, I won't."

Emma and Janie opened their magazines again. Janie started to cut right away, but Emma couldn't find another picture she liked. She wished Carmen would come home early. She could hardly wait to tell her about the baby. And Carmen would be glad to hear that Emma wasn't going to move away yet.

"Emma," said Janie. "I found a picture for you. Look. It's a bedroom." Janie held her magazine out.

Emma took it from her.

"See?" Janie was smiling as if she'd found something really great.

It *was* a picture of a bedroom. A yucky boy's bedroom. "Thanks," said Emma. "It's nice." She ripped the page out. How could Janie think she'd like this dumb picture— ugly curtains, football trophies on the shelves, boring green blankets on the bunk beds . . .

Wait! Emma stared at the picture. Bunk beds! That was the answer.

≫ 12 ≪

Emma looked at the picture of the boy's bedroom. But she wasn't really seeing it. In her mind she saw a different bedroom. The bunk beds had pretty new blankets, blue on the top for herself and pink on the bottom for Janie. And across the room she saw a little white crib. In the crib was her new baby sister.

"Hey, Janie," said Emma, "this picture is really great. You know why?"

"Why?" said Janie. She stopped cutting.

"Because it just gave me the best idea."

Janie waited.

"Look again," said Emma. "It's the bunk beds!"

"So?" Janie picked up her scissors.

"Don't you *see?*" said Emma. "If *we* got bunk beds, you and me, then we could both have the baby in our room. Her crib could fit too."

"Oh," said Janie. "Bunk beds. Let me see it again."

Emma passed the picture over to her.

"I call top bunk," said Janie.

Emma grabbed the picture back. "I need this," she said, "to show Mommy. And *I* get top bunk. It was my idea."

Mrs. Tucker came into the kitchen. "What idea?" she said.

Emma and Janie both started talking at the same time. Emma tried to talk louder. "I want to tell her," she yelled.

"Shhhhh," said her mother. "Nick is sleeping. Now, you can both tell me—one at a time. Emma first."

"No fair," Janie whined.

"I had this great idea. . . ." Emma started. And she told her mother about the bunk beds.

"But *I* found the picture," said Janie. "And *I* called top bunk first."

Emma and Janie waited to see what their mother would say.

"I don't know, girls." Mrs. Tucker shook her head slowly. "It's a good idea, but I just don't know if we can afford—"

Emma had been holding her breath. She let it out now. "But *Mommy!*" she cried.

"I'm not saying no. But I don't want you to get too excited about this until we've asked your father. Bunk beds would cost a lot of money."

Emma groaned. Couldn't her mother see how important this was? There just had to be a way to get them.

"I don't want to do scrapbooks anymore," said Janie. "Let's do something else."

"Who's talking about scrapbooks?" cried Emma. "Don't you even care about the bunk beds?"

"Emma," said her mother. "Calm down. You might as well stop talking about them for now. We'll see what Daddy says tonight."

"Well . . . okay," said Emma. "But I'm not going to stop *thinking* about them."

"Let's play hide-and-seek," said Janie. "I hide first."

"Okay," Emma agreed.

"Wait a minute," said their mother. "Can't you think of a quiet game? Nick is—"

"We'll be quiet," said Emma. Now that Janie could really count and didn't always hide in the same place, it was fun to play hide-and-seek with her.

"Well, all right," said her mother, "if you can play quietly."

"We'll be really, really, *really* quiet," Emma promised. She and Janie ran into the living room before their mother could change her mind. "These are the rules," she told Janie. "Count to one hundred, no yelling, run only with bare feet, stay away from Nick's room. Okay?"

"Okay," said Janie. "And I hide first."

They both pulled their sandals off. Then Emma hid her face in a corner and started counting. She counted to one hundred. "Ready or not, here I come." She turned around and looked. Janie wasn't in the living room. She never hid there. Emma peeked behind the corner chair just in case. Then she headed for the kitchen.

Mrs. Tucker was sitting at the table with a glass of lemonade. She was writing a letter. "Is Janie in here?" asked Emma.

"Janie who?" said her mother.

There was a small giggle from the far side of the stove. Emma ran over and tapped Janie. "You're it."

"No fair," cried Janie. "Mommy made me laugh." But she followed Emma into the living room.

"Don't peek," said Emma. "And don't skip any numbers." She waited until Janie started counting. Then she ran out of the room. She knew just where she wanted to hide.

Emma ran down the hall. She stopped at the linen closet. The closet had no door, but her mother had hung a long curtain across the doorway. Emma pushed the curtain aside.

The top shelves were full of winter clothes in plastic bags, and the lower shelves held sheets and towels. But between the lowest shelf and the floor was a space that was perfect for hiding. Emma pulled an old suitcase out. She crawled into the closet and pulled the suitcase back in front of her. Just in time.

"Ready or not, here I come," Janie called. And then it was quiet.

Emma settled down to wait. At first she sat with her back against one wall, but the shelf above her was too low. Her head pressed against it. She let herself slide down until she was lying on the floor, her knees pulled up, her bare feet pressed against the opposite wall. That was better. It was nice in here—like a little house . . . or maybe a bunk bed.

She looked up at the shelf. She pretended that it was her bedroom ceiling and that she was up in her new top bunk. Maybe she would paint some stars on the ceiling. She could hang her favorite pictures along the wall. She could keep books up there, on a shelf, and a flashlight and some paper and pencils. It would be great. *If* her father said yes about the bunk beds.

Emma looked around her in the dim light. It was fun hiding in the closet. She would have to keep this place a secret. Then she could come here sometimes when she wasn't playing hide-and-seek—when she just wanted to be alone.

She sat up slowly so she wouldn't bang her head. Now she just had to wait until she was sure Janie wouldn't see her. Then she could crawl out and run for home base. Emma listened. Janie was still in the kitchen. She was talking with her mother.

The doorbell rang. Emma heard Janie run out of the kitchen. She heard her say "Who's there?"

Emma pushed the suitcase aside and crawled out of the closet. No one saw her. She raced down the hall. "Home free," she called as she skidded into the living room.

"No fair," yelled Janie. She came running into the room. Carmen was with her.

"Carmen!" cried Emma. "You're back."

"We just got home," said Carmen. "My mother says you can hold Felicia. Can you come over now?"

"I think so," said Emma. She scooped up her sandals and ran into the kitchen. "Mommy," she said. "Can I go to Carmen's? Her mother said I can hold Felicia."

"Go ahead, Emma," said her mother. "But don't stay too long. Be back before supper."

Emma buckled her sandals. "I'll be back early," she promised.

"Mommy," said Janie. "I want to go too."

"You can help me make Jell-O," said her mother.

Emma pulled Carmen toward the door. She couldn't wait to hold Felicia. She couldn't wait to tell Carmen about the new baby, and the bunk bed idea.

≫ 13 ≪

"So," said Emma, "if we get bunk beds, then there will be plenty of space for a crib in our room."

"Right," said Carmen.

Emma and Carmen were sitting on the couch in Carmen's apartment.

Emma was holding Felicia on her lap. The baby looked up at her and made a little cooing sound.

"Oh, look, Carmen. She likes me. She's trying to talk to me."

Carmen smiled. "She's a smart baby."

Felicia cooed again. She kicked her legs.

Emma touched one of her little bare feet. The tiny toenails had pink polish on them. "I hope my mother lets me put nail polish on *my* baby."

"But she doesn't even let you and Janie wear it," said Carmen. "And anyway, you might get a boy baby."

"Don't *say* that," cried Emma. "It's just got to be a girl."

"Well, I hope it's a girl, but—"

"Let's talk about something else," said Emma. "Do you want to come up in my new bunk bed if we get them?"

"Okay," said Carmen. "But what can we do up there?"

"It's going to be fun," said Emma. "We can draw or play checkers or read. . . . We can do lots of things." She told Carmen all about how she was going to fix her bunk up.

"It sounds kind of like a clubhouse," said Carmen.

"That's a great idea!" Emma wished she had thought of it herself. "Let's make it *be* a clubhouse. A private one, for just the two of us."

"You're so lucky," said Carmen. "A new baby *and* bunk beds."

"I *think* bunk beds. My father has to say yes first." Emma could see her new clubhouse disappearing and her father saying, "I'm sorry, Emma, but bunk beds would cost too much. . . ." Emma blinked her eyes. It would be terrible if he said no.

Felicia started to cry. Emma rocked her gently, but she cried louder.

Mrs. Perez came into the room. She took the baby from Emma. "There, there, sweetheart," she said, patting her back. "You're hungry and tired. I know."

Emma and Carmen stood up. "I guess I should go home now," said Emma. "My mother told me not to stay too long."

Mrs. Perez rocked Felicia. "Tell your mother and father I think it's wonderful news about the baby, Emma."

"I will. And thank you for letting me hold Felicia."

Carmen walked Emma out to the elevator. "When are you going to find out about the bunk beds?"

"I don't know," said Emma. "Maybe my

father is home already. Maybe my mother already asked him. What am I going to do if he says no?"

"He won't," said Carmen. "You really *need* bunk beds."

"I'll die if he says no," Emma cried.

The elevator door opened. Emma stepped in.

"Good luck," said Carmen.

The elevator door slid shut. Emma crossed her fingers. "I hope. . . ." she said to herself. "I hope, I hope, I hope."

≫ 14 ≪

Emma pushed her apartment door open. "Is Daddy home?" she yelled.

"Hello, Emma," her mother called back from the kitchen.

Nick came out to meet her. "Potty," he said. He took her hand.

"Potty?" Emma thought she must be hearing wrong.

Nick pulled her. "Potty." There was no mistake.

Emma couldn't believe it. She went into the kitchen still holding Nick's hand.

Mrs. Tucker and Janie were setting the table.

"Is Daddy home?" Emma asked again. "And what's going on with Nick?"

Nick was trying to pull Emma out of the kitchen.

"Daddy's not home yet," said her mother. "And Nick wants to use the potty because . . ." She stopped.

"It's not fair," said Janie. "Mommy says Nick can have a jelly bean every time he uses the potty."

"Jelly bean," said Nick. He had a big smile on his face.

"Not fair," whined Janie.

Emma started to giggle.

Her mother was laughing too. "Oh, Emma," she said.

"It's *not* funny," said Janie. She stamped her foot.

Mrs. Tucker tried to stop laughing. "Emma, please take Nick to the bathroom."

"But why can't he go by himself?" asked Emma. "He knows how."

"Because he doesn't get a jelly bean unless he *does* something in the potty, so you have to look. And you can wash your hands for dinner while you're there."

"Oh, brother," said Emma. But she let Nick lead her down the hall to the bathroom.

Nick settled himself on his potty.

Emma washed her hands. Then she sat down on the edge of the bathtub to wait. "Hurry up," she said. She thought she heard the front door opening.

"Can't," said Nick.

Emma stood up. "I'll be back in a minute."

"*No,*" screamed Nick.

"Okay, okay." Emma sat down again. "But you better hurry."

Finally Nick stood up. "All done," he said proudly. "See?"

Emma looked. There were about two drops in the potty. "Good job," she said. "You get a jelly bean."

Emma left Nick pulling up his pants. She raced down the hall to the kitchen.

Her father was there, looking in the refrigerator. Janie was sitting at the table. Mrs. Tucker turned from the stove. "The hamburgers are almost ready," she said. "Where's Nick, Emma?"

"He's finished. He's coming. Did you ask

Daddy?" Emma was so nervous she could hardly stand it. She looked at her father's back.

"Ask me about what?" said Mr. Tucker. "I can't find the ketchup."

Nick came running into the kitchen. "Jelly bean, jelly bean," he yelled. His shorts were twisted around his waist.

"Come here, Nick," said Mrs. Tucker. "Let me fix your pants."

"I want bunk beds too," said Janie. "And I want the top one."

"No way," yelled Emma. "I want—"

The refrigerator door slammed. Mr. Tucker turned around. "Do you know what *I* want?" he said in a loud voice. "I want all three of you to be quiet." He looked at Nick and Janie and Emma, one at a time. "Now I'm going to wash up for dinner. And when I come back, nobody had better ask me for one single thing." He walked stiffly out of the room.

Emma thought that even her father's foot-steps sounded angry. She waited until she

heard the bathroom door slam. Suddenly the kitchen was too quiet. Emma felt a little scared. "What's the matter with Daddy?" she said.

≫15≪

Emma looked at her mother. "Did you ask Daddy about the bunk beds? Is that why he's angry?"

Her mother picked Nick up and put him in his high chair. "No," she said. "I didn't."

"Jelly bean," said Nick in a small voice.

Mrs. Tucker got three jelly beans from a big glass jar. She gave one to Nick, one to Janie, and one to Emma. "Listen, Emma," she said. "I don't think tonight will be a good time to ask Daddy about the beds. He's had a bad day at work, and he doesn't feel too well. Okay?"

Emma popped her jelly bean into her mouth. She didn't say anything. She didn't want to wait another day. Waiting was too hard. Maybe her father would feel better after dinner. Then she would ask him about the bunk beds herself. Maybe she could even cheer him up right now.

Mr. Tucker came back into the kitchen. He sat down at the table.

Emma sat down too. "Hi, Daddy," she said. She smiled at him. She tried to make her face look cheerful.

"Hi, Emma," he answered. He even smiled back a little.

Emma looked at him carefully. She thought he looked better already.

Everybody was quiet during dinner. Emma watched her father. He didn't really look angry anymore. But he ate quickly, without talking. Every time he looked up, Emma smiled at him.

"Who wants dessert?" said Mrs. Tucker.

"Me," said Nick and Janie.

"Me, please," said Emma.

"No thanks," said their father. He pushed his chair back. "I'm going to watch the news." He took his coffee out of the kitchen.

Emma heard the TV go on. "I changed

my mind," she said. "I don't want any dessert. May I be excused?"

"All right," said her mother. She passed bowls of red Jell-O to Janie and Nick.

Emma went into the living room. She sat down quietly next to her father on the couch. She knew this would be the only time she'd be alone with him. "Daddy—" she said.

"Not now, Emma. The news is coming on."

Emma hated the news. It was the most boring thing on TV. She hoped a commercial would come on soon. She hoped Janie and Nick wouldn't finish their Jell-O before then. Emma settled back to wait.

The news went on and on. She didn't listen to it. She thought about the new bunk beds instead. The clubhouse was a great idea. She and Carmen could keep the club things on the shelf at the head of her bed. They would need a notebook to write down rules. Emma wasn't sure what else they would need. Maybe a box with a lock to keep secret things in.

It was going to be a wonderful clubhouse. And at night, when she was alone in bed, Emma could look down and see her little baby sister asleep in her crib.

Finally a commercial came on. "Daddy," said Emma.

"Mmmm." Her father was still looking at the television. He wasn't paying attention to her.

"I have to ask you something important," said Emma.

Her father frowned a little, but he stopped staring at the TV.

Emma saw the frown. Maybe she should wait. Maybe her mother was right.

"Go ahead," said her father. "I'm listening."

Emma took a deep breath. "Well, you know," she said, "we're going to have a baby. . . ."

"Yes, I know that."

"And if it's a girl," Emma went on, "Janie and I wanted to have her in our room, or even if it's a boy, but we hope it's going to be a girl, but our room is too crowded, so I had this really great idea, and, uh . . ."

"Well?" said her father.

"Well," said Emma, "I was thinking that if Janie and I got new bunk beds, we'd have plenty of space in our room and . . ."

"No," said her father. "I'm sorry, Emma, but if it costs money, I don't want to hear about it." He turned back to the TV.

Emma felt as if her father had slapped her. She had known that he might say no. But deep down inside she hadn't thought he really would. Bunk beds were such a *good* idea. And he wouldn't even listen. He just said no.

Emma jumped up from the couch. "I . . . I hate you!" she cried. Then she turned and ran out of the room.

"Emma, come back here, right now," yelled her father.

But Emma didn't answer. She pounded down the hall and into the bathroom. Then she slammed the door and locked it. She was breathing hard. Tears burned her eyes.

It just wasn't fair. No house, no bedroom, no puppy, and now no bunk beds.

There was a knock on the bathroom door.

Emma didn't answer. She knew that her voice would have that funny, half-crying sound. She reached over and flushed the toilet.

"Emma, are you in there?" It was her mother. "Answer me."

"Go away," said Emma.

The doorknob rattled. "Emma, open the door. I want to talk to you."

"No," said Emma. She wished she could hide or escape.

"Emma, your father is very upset. I want you to come out now and apologize to him."

"*He's* upset?" cried Emma. "What about me? Doesn't anybody care how I feel?"

"Oh, Emma."

"*You* even said getting bunk beds was a good idea. And I told Carmen we were getting them, and we were going to have a private clubhouse, and now . . ."

"Oh, Emma," her mother said again. "I know you're disappointed, but you still can't talk to Daddy that way."

"But it's true!" cried Emma. "I *do* hate him."

"It's not true," said her mother. "And you know Daddy loves you very much. He didn't say no bunk beds to hurt you."

"Then why—"

"Emma, you know why. I told you that we might not be able to afford them."

"I know," said Emma. She didn't want to admit it, but her mother *had* warned her.

"So, come out now and tell Daddy you're sorry. Okay?"

Emma didn't answer.

"Okay?" her mother repeated.

Emma knew she had to give in. She looked at herself in the mirror over the sink. Her face was red. So were her eyes. "I . . . I have to wash my hands first," she said. "Then I will."

"All right," said her mother. "I'll be in the kitchen."

Emma turned the water on. She washed her face and dried it three times. She still looked terrible.

She opened the bathroom door and went down the hall to the living room.

Janie and Nick were sitting next to their father on the couch. "Emma's face is all red," said Janie.

Emma gave her a dirty look. "I apologize," she said to her father.

"What did Emma do?" Janie asked.

"Never mind, Janie," said her father. "It's over now. Right, Emma?"

"Right," she said. But she didn't mean it. She was still angry.

≫ 16 ≪

Emma went into the kitchen. "I did it," she said to her mother. "I apologized."

"Good. Now, why don't you and Janie go out for a while?"

"I don't want to," said Emma.

"Are you sure? It must be cooler outside."

"I'm sure." Emma left the kitchen. But she didn't go back into the living room. Instead she ran on tiptoe down the hall. She stopped at the linen closet and looked behind her. Nobody was there. Quickly she pulled the curtain aside. She dragged the suitcase out and crawled into her secret hiding place. Then she tugged the suitcase in after her.

It was hot in the closet, but Emma didn't

mind. She wanted to be alone. She slid down until her back was on the floor and her knees were scrunched up. She looked at the shelf above her in the dim light. For a long time, Emma didn't move.

It would serve them right if something terrible happened to me, she thought. If I got very, very sick or if I even died. They'd really be sorry then. Emma pictured her family standing around her grave. Her mother was crying. So were Janie and Nick.

Her father was saying, "My poor child. She never got to live in a house or have a dog or bunk beds. If only I'd known. Now it's too late." Then he started crying too.

Emma felt tears stinging her eyes. It was so sad. Her whole family was crying. But she wasn't dead. She was right here. She had to let them know.

Emma wiped her tears away with her hand. Then she shoved the suitcase aside and scrambled out of the closet. She ran down the hall and burst into the living room.

"Here I am!" she cried.

Her mother and father were sitting on the couch. Janie and Nick were on the floor. They all looked up at Emma. They were not crying. They looked surprised, not sad.

Emma stood there staring at them. She felt confused and embarrassed.

Nobody said anything for a moment.

Finally Emma said, "Didn't someone call me?" She couldn't tell them what had really happened. It would be better to pretend.

"No," her mother answered. "No one called."

"Oh," said Emma. "Well, I guess I'll go back to my room." She turned to leave.

"Wait for me," said Janie.

Emma started down the hall.

Janie caught up with her. "I know about the bunk beds," she said sadly. "Mommy and Daddy were talking about it. I listened."

Emma didn't say anything. She went into

her room and threw herself down on her bed.

Janie sat on her little chair. "Maybe we don't need bunk beds," she said. "Maybe if we move the furniture a different way, there'll be room for a crib."

"There won't," said Emma. But she sat up and looked around.

"We could push our beds together," said Janie. "And the crib could go—"

"Forget it," said Emma. "Can't you see, there's just not enough room?"

The doorbell rang.

"Emma," her mother called. "It's Carmen."

"I'm coming," Emma yelled back.

"Can I come with you?" asked Janie. "Please."

"Well," said Emma, "I guess so. If you don't bother us." After all, Emma thought, Janie *had* been trying to be helpful about the room.

"I won't bother you," said Janie. She followed Emma down the hall.

Carmen was waiting at the front door.

"Don't go too far, girls," said their mother. "It's getting late."

"We won't." Emma went out into the hall. Carmen and Janie followed.

As soon as they were outside, Carmen said, "Did you find out about the bunk beds?"

Emma sat down on one of the front steps. "My father said no."

"Oh, that's too bad." Carmen sat down beside Emma.

Janie sat down next to Carmen. "He said new bunk beds would be too much money. I heard him tell my mother."

They were all quiet for a moment, thinking about the bunk beds.

Then the door behind them opened. Janie's friend Keesha came out. She was holding a jump rope with red handles. "Hi, Janie," she said. "Want to take turns?" She held the rope out.

Janie looked longingly at the jump rope.

"Go ahead," said Emma. "We'll watch."

That was all Janie needed. She jumped up and ran down the steps. Soon she and Keesha were taking turns with the jump rope.

Emma and Carmen sat together. "Do you want to do something?" asked Carmen.

Emma looked around. There were a lot of kids out. Some were on skateboards, some were playing tag, and she could see a group of older girls jumping double dutch on the other side of the parking lot. "No." She sighed. "I don't feel like doing anything."

Carmen sighed too.

"You know," Emma said after a moment, "it's really not fair. I know that new bunk beds would cost a lot of money, but—"

Carmen cut in. "Emma, did you ask your father for *new* bunk beds?"

"You know I did. What do you mean?"

"I mean," said Carmen, "that maybe you made a mistake."

Emma looked at her as if she were crazy.

"Don't you remember when our old kitchen table broke, and we had to get another one?"

"Yes," said Emma.

"Well, we didn't get a brand-new one. We got one secondhand."

"Hey," said Emma. "I never thought of that. Secondhand wouldn't cost so much, would it? And you can fix up secondhand things with paint, right?"

"Right," said Carmen.

Emma and Carmen smiled at each other.

Janie came over and stood panting before Emma. "Do you and Carmen want a turn?" she said. "We're getting tired."

"Sure," said Emma.

The four girls took turns jumping until they were all hot and tired. Emma was thinking about getting secondhand bunk beds the whole time. Her father *couldn't* say no if the beds didn't cost much money. And if they were painted with shiny white paint they'd probably look as good as new. Maybe she could even help with the painting herself.

Mrs. Tucker came outside. "Time to come in, girls."

"Good luck," Carmen whispered to Emma.

"Thanks," said Emma. Then she and Janie followed their mother indoors.

≫ 17 ≪

"Time for your bath, girls," said their mother. "I already ran the water."

"Okay," said Emma. "But first I have to tell Daddy something—private."

"Me too," said Janie.

"Emma," her mother said, "you're not going to ask Daddy about getting bunk beds again, are you? Because—"

"I'm not," said Emma. "Really."

"Well, okay then. Go ahead. Janie will be waiting for you in the tub."

"Not fair," Janie whined, but she went off down the hall.

Emma found her father in the kitchen. He had a lot of papers spread out on the table. "Bills," he said, pointing at the papers.

"I'm not going to ask you for bunk beds again," Emma said quickly.

"That's a relief," said her father.

"I just wanted to tell you something," she went on. "I wanted to tell you that Carmen's new kitchen table isn't new."

"It's not?" Her father looked confused.

"No," said Emma. "It's *secondhand*."

"Oh," said Mr. Tucker, after a moment. "I think I see."

Emma waited for her father to say something else, but he didn't. "Well, I guess I'll go take my bath," she said.

"Okay. And I'll get back to these bills."

Emma walked slowly out of the kitchen. She stopped in the doorway. "Good night, Daddy. *Secondhand* means not so much money, you know."

"Good night, Emma. I'll think about that."

There was nothing else to say. Emma went down the hall to the bathroom.

"What did you tell Daddy?" Janie asked.

"Nothing important," said Emma as she

climbed into the tub. She didn't want to tell Janie now. She'd let her know when her father said yes. *If* he said yes.

Later, when they had finished their bath and had their story and the light was turned off, Janie asked again. "Why won't you tell me what you said to Daddy?"

"I'll tell you tomorrow," Emma said. "I promise."

"Okay," said Janie. "Good night." She yawned. Soon she was sucking her thumb.

Emma yawned too, but something was wrong. She felt sad, but she didn't know why. She lay on her back listening to the night sounds, Janie sucking her thumb, the TV buzzing, cars going by out on the street.

Emma stretched. Then she pulled her legs up and hugged them to her chest, the way she had when she was in the linen closet. Suddenly she knew what was making her sad. It was the half-dream she'd had in the closet.

She remembered how her whole family had been crying because they thought she

was dead. Even her father had cried. Then
Emma remembered how she'd yelled at her
father before that. Yelled *I hate you* when
he wouldn't listen to her bunk bed idea.
But I don't hate you, Daddy, Emma
thought. I really don't.

Emma sat up and swung her legs over
the side of her bed. She knew what she had
to do. In the dim light from the hall, she
found a piece of paper on Janie's table and
a crayon. She carried them over near her
door, where she could see better.

Then she sat down on the floor and
started to write.

Dear Daddy,

*I do not hate you. I was mad
about the beds. That's why I said it.
But it isn't true. Even if we never get
the bunk beds, I love you and
Mommy and even Janie and Nick.*

*Love,
Emma*

Emma read the letter over. It looked messy because of the crayon, but it said the right thing. She folded it and wrote *To Daddy* on the outside. Then she tiptoed into her parents' room and put it on her father's pillow.

Emma ran back to her own room and jumped into bed. I did it, she thought. She felt much better. And then she heard footsteps coming down the hall.

"Emma," said her father, "was that you I just heard?"

"Yes," said Emma. "But I'm going to sleep right now. I promise."

"Shhh." Her father put a finger to his lips. "Come with me," he said quietly.

Emma got out of bed and followed him out to the living room.

Her mother was sitting on the couch. Her father sat down too. He motioned for Emma to sit between them.

"Emma," said her mother, "we've been talking, and we thought you should know what Daddy and I decided."

"What?" said Emma nervously.

"Well," said her mother, "we think that things haven't been too easy for you the last few days, and we haven't been very helpful."

"You mean about the baby?" said Emma.

"Well, yes," said her father. "Mommy says you've been very grown-up about understanding why we can't afford to move right now. And she says you've been trying to get along better with Janie and Nick too. So . . ."

Emma held her breath.

"So," her father repeated. "We think that getting secondhand bunk beds is the least we can do for you."

"Oh," Emma breathed. "Really?" She almost couldn't believe it.

"Really," said her father. He smiled.

Emma threw her arms around him and hugged him. Then she hugged her mother. "I love you," she said.

"We love you too," said her mother. "Now, off you go to bed."

"Okay," said Emma. "Thank you for tell-

ing me about the bunk beds tonight. See you in the morning." She ran down the hall to her bedroom. She got into bed. Then she remembered the letter to her father. Should she go get it?

Emma smiled to herself. No. She would leave the letter where it was. She still wanted her father to know that she loved him, bunk beds or no bunk beds.

Emma settled back against her pillow.

In the morning she would tell Janie about the bunk beds. She could hardly wait to tell Carmen. She smiled again. Everything was going to work out just fine.